FATHER and SON

For the angelic host of FCB
—G. M.

Text copyright © 2006 by Geraldine McCaughrean
Illustrations copyright © 2006 by Fabian Negrin

First published by Hodder Children's Books in 2006
First U.S. edition, 2006

Printed in China

1 3 5 7 9 10 8 6 4 2
Library of Congress Cataloging-in-Publication Data on file.
Reinforced binding
ISBN 1-4231-0344-0
Visit www.hyperionbooksforchildren.com

FATHER and SON
A NATIVITY STORY

GERALDINE McCAUGHREAN

Illustrations by

FABIAN NEGRIN

Hyperion Books for Children

NEW YORK

AFTER THE STAR had set, after the angels had roosted, after the shepherds had hurried back to their sheep, there was one person still awake in the dark stable.

Joseph sat watching the baby asleep in a manger of straw.

"Mine, but not mine," he whispered. "How am I supposed to stand in for your real Father? How is a simple man like me to bring up the Son of God?

"Not a good start. I could not even find him a proper place to be born, a proper bed to sleep in— he who has cradled us all in his hands since the Start of Time.

"What lullabies should I sing to someone who taught the angels to dance and peppered the sky with songbirds?

"How can I teach him his words and letters: he who strung the alphabet together, he who whispered dreams into a million, million ears, in a thousand different languages?

"The very thought of it leaves me speechless.

"How can I teach him the Scriptures? It will be like reading him a book he wrote himself!

"What stories can I tell him? He wrote the whole history of the world.

"What jokes? He knows them all.

"Didn't he invent the hilarious hippopotamus and make the rivers gurgle with laughter?

"Didn't he form the first face, wink, and make it smile?

"Someone tell me: how do
I protect a child whose arm
brandished the first bolt of
lightning, who lobbed the first
thunderclap, who wears sunlight
for armor, and a helmet of stars?

"And yet…and yet…somehow
my heart quakes for you, child,
small as you are.

"How shall I teach you Right and Wrong, when it was YOU who drew up the rules, YOU who parted Good from Bad?

"How?

"When I get angry and lose my temper, who will be to blame? Always me, I suppose.

"How do I feed and clothe someone who seeded the oceans with fish and hung up fruit in the trees? Who shod the camels and crowned the deer?

"It's bread and fishes from now on, son, and clothes no better than mine.

"What games shall we play,
boy, you and I? I mean, how can
I rough-and-tumble with someone
who pinned the ocean in place
with a single, tack-headed moon?

"And how shall I ever astound you, child, as my father did me? You are the one who fitted the chicken into the egg and the oak tree into an acorn!

"How can I put a roof over your head, knowing it was you who glass-roofed the world and thatched the sky with clouds, and stitched the snow with threads of melting silver?

"I am a carpenter, child. By
rights, you should learn my trade.
But how can I teach you to plane
a door, knowing it was you who
planed the plains, who carved the
valleys and hewed the hills, the
wind in your one hand and rain
in the other?

"How?

"What presents can I offer
you who has already given me
everything?
This wife.
This night.
This happiness.
This son.

"What shall I pass down to you,
little one, apart from a world of
Love? Not as much as the color
of my eyes. Not even my name.

"And yet... I've been thinking,
child...

"My hands
are strong,
God knows.
And everyone
needs an
extra pair
of hands
from time
to time.

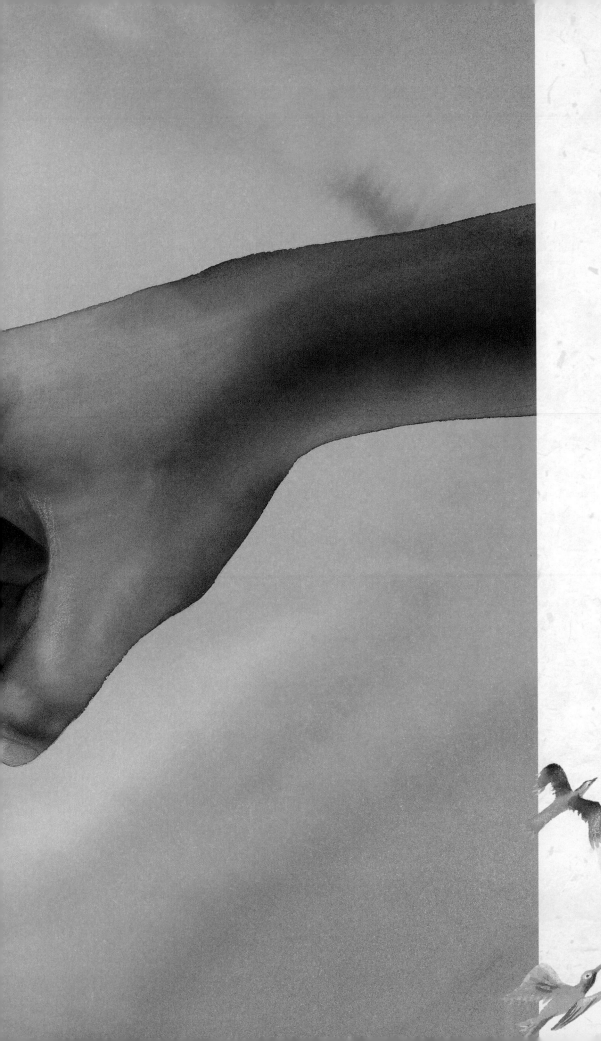

"So that's what I'll give you, son. That's what I'll be, God willing. A helping hand."

So, long after the star had set,
after the angels had roosted,
after the shepherds had hurried
back to their sheep, there was
one person still awake in the dark
stable, watching over a sleeping
child...

...while his God watched over him.

AUTHOR'S NOTE

THE NATIVITY STORY tells us what Mary felt, but only what Joseph dreamed. It tells us Mary's thoughts on receiving gifts of gold, frankincense, and myrrh; not what Joseph felt at receiving the gift of a stepson. His is a strange, half-glimpsed story.

Never in his life did Joseph have to grapple with the difficult notion of The Trinity: of God, Jesus, and the Holy Spirit being three in one. Joseph was already dead when, thirty years later, Jesus spoke the amazing secret out loud . . . "I and the Father are one."

But how, after such an extraordinary beginning, could Joseph *not* have realized that the boy in his care was in some way divine? That was the thought which gave rise to this book: That one night—and on many more, I dare say—Joseph the carpenter must have held his God in the crook of his arm, and sung Him to sleep.